MW00761808

Save the Three Little Pigs!

adapted by Melinda R
based on the screenplay by Sascha Paladino
illustrated by Alexandria Fogarty, Little Airplane Productions

SIMON SPOTLIGHT/NICKELODEON
New York   London   Toronto   Sydney

SIMON SPOTLIGHT
An imprint of Simon & Schuster Children's Publishing Division
1230 Avenue of the Americas, New York, New York 10020
Manufactured in the United States of America
First Edition
2 4 6 8 10 9 7 5 3 1
Library of Congress Cataloging-in-Publication Data
Richards, Melinda.
Save the three little pigs! / adapted by Melinda Richards ; illustrated by
Little Airplane Productions. — 1st ed.
p. cm. — (Ready-to-read)
"Based on the TV series Nick Jr. Wonder Pets! as seen on Nick Jr."
ISBN: 978-1-4169-7198-6
I. Little Airplane Productions II. Wonder pets! (Television program)
III. Title.
PZ7.R39245Sav 2009
[E]—dc22
2008022781

Linny!

Tuck!

And Ming-Ming, too!

We are the Wonder Pets!

Look!

We see three little pigs.

A wolf is chasing them!

Look!

This little pig is making

a house of straw.

Huff! Puff!

The wolf blew the house down!

Run!

This little pig is making

a house of sticks.

Huff! Puff!

The wolf blew the house down!

This little pig is making

a house of flowers.

The wolf will blow this house

down too!

The pigs need a stronger house!

We can use bricks!

Huff! Puff!

The pigs are safe!

This calls for some celery!